IVY

A FOSTERING HOPE BOOK

Written by Kelly Krout

Illustrated by Kyra Krout

Cover art and Illustrations by Kyra Krout

Interior layout and design by Megan Meredith

Synopsis: It's a long process for Ivy and Wes to find their forever family, but it's worth the wait. Learn about what adoption through foster care can look like as you follow their story. Sometimes even the saddest beginnings can have happy endings.

Published 2019
A Herald's Megaphone Publishing Ltd. Co.

megaphonebooks.com

ISBN: 9781733755641

To the children waiting for their forever homes.

Kate and Paul had lived with the Hales

since last September,

It'd been so long, she was sure Paul couldn't remember

That Kate used to be the one who took care of her brother,

She'd rocked him and fed him and been

like a mother.

She remembered what happened
when they'd been taken away.

She would never forget that awful day.

She'd held Paul all day in the office.

All the grown-ups had said that she was so cautious.

She'd carefully bounced him up and down on her leg,

While a worker made phone calls and said, "Hi, it's Meg!"

"I have two kids here needing beds, do you have any space?

Yes, I think this will be a longer-term case."

She didn't know what that meant exactly at the time,

But somehow, she knew she and Paul would be fine.

After listening to Meg make call after call,

She took him for walks up and down the hall.

Meg peeked her head out, "I told you not to worry!

Grab your bag and your brother, come on, let's hurry!"

Kate put on her backpack and picked up baby Paul,

She knew how to make him feel **safe**,

even though she was **small**.

Kate was only six, but she seemed much older.

"You're little, but fierce!" adults had told her.

That first night at the Hales, Paul just wouldn't sleep,

Until Kate tucked him in, then **not a peep**.

After a bit Kate and Paul got more settled in,

Kate was **always helping** to make Paul grin.

Kate showed Mrs. Hale how to do her silly wiggle,

That always had a way of making Paul giggle.

They told Kate **not to worry** so much about her brother,

But they loved how much they protected each other.

They would say, "Be a kid, go on and play!

We will watch Paul, it's a **beautiful day!**"

She learned how to swing high and do a cartwheel.

She learned to ride a bike -

That was a big deal!

She started to trust the Hales to take care of Paul,

It's fun to just be a kid, after all.

Fall turned to winter....

and winter to spring...

By then Paul was getting into everything!

He'd learned how to crawl, then quickly to walk.

Kate and the Hales loved it when he tried to talk.

Kate felt weird when Paul called the Hales Mom and Dad.

He was happy,
                    but it made her feel kind of sad.

She hadn't seen her parents in so long.

Calling other people Mom and Dad felt wrong.

But she liked the Hales too. She **liked them a lot**.

"Maybe I can just stay here…" Kate often thought.

She did love and miss her old family, that was still true.

But maybe she could love another family too.

The case worker told Kate as the leaves started to fall,

"I'm afraid you won't

be going back home after all."

Kate was sad but deep down already knew that was true.

But she still didn't really know what to do.

The Hales asked her one day,

"Can we **adopt** you, Kate?

You and Paul can stay here forever,
it could be great!

We would love to be your mom and dad,

Being a family forever
would make us so very glad."

Kate actually loved the idea and said yes right away!

It made her heart happy to be able to stay.

She asked, "Can Paul and I each change our name?"

They said, "Yes! And our last names can be the same!"

She'd always loved the name Ivy

and thought that would be neat,

And she thought the name Wes for her brother was sweet.

Changing names felt like a new beginning.

When she called herself Ivy she couldn't stop grinning.

When adoption day came,

the ground was covered in snow.

The sun on the white made everything glow.

They went into the courtroom
and the judge said with a smile,

"Kate and Paul, I haven't seen you in a while!

I hear you'd like your names to be new.

And I love the names you've chosen too!

So I declare you, Ivy, and your brother, Wes,

Welcome to your new family,

I wish you the best!"

So it was official! The Hale family of four!

Not one of them could have asked for more.

Ivy knew from the beginning they'd be okay,

Adoption made them a family that day.

THE END

If you are worried that a child is not safe, please call the child abuse hotline.

For your state and their reporting hotlines, please visit:

https://www.nccafv.org/child-abuse-reporting-numbers

Kyra Krout is Kelly's 18 year old niece and recent High School graduate. She enjoys water coloring what she sees in nature.

Made in the USA
Middletown, DE
23 November 2020